# COLORS OF THE MAGICAL CASTLE

Copyright © 2022 Sheryl Bailey
Published By: Universal Reads
All rights reserved.

Tracy and Lily were the best of friends.
The two girls lived in a small town called Havilah.
Tracy was a smart girl, always eager to learn new things.
Lily, on the other hand, was more of a dreamer.
She hardly paid attention to any of her lessons in school.
Instead, she looked out of the classroom window
and imagined lots of things.
Lily often imagined that the small,
quiet town had transformed into a magical castle.

One afternoon,
Tracy and Lily were walking home from school
when a peaceful lake appeared.
The two girls were taken aback!
They had taken this route to school many times before
but had never seen the lake.

"Lily, I don't think I've ever seen this lake before.
I didn't even see it this morning," Tracy said.
Lily knelt down by the lake.
She was so curious about it that she wanted to touch it.
No sooner had Lily touched the water, she disappeared!

Tracy was terrified. Where had Lily gone?
Tracy called Lily's name,
but she didn't get any response.

As she continued to call Lily's name,
she also tried searching for her;
when she tripped over a tree stump close to the lake
and stumbled in.
When Tracy fell into the water,
she felt as if something strange had happened to her.
She could no longer see anything and all she heard were strange noises.

When the strange noises stopped, Tracy could see once again.
She was no longer at the lake side.
Now, she was in a very big castle.
In the castle everything was red, green, blue, and yellow.
When Tracy spotted Lily, the two girls immediately embraced.
They were so happy to see each other.
"What is this place, Lily?
All I can remember is tripping and falling into the water.

I can't remember how I got here," Tracy said.
"Be quiet, Tracy. I can hear footsteps.
I think this place is a magical castle,"
Lily whispered.
The footsteps got louder.
But before either of the girls could move,
they were surrounded by guards dressed in bright yellow
uniforms.

"Take them and lock them up in the dungeon,"
a tall guard instructed. Tracy and Lily were terrified.
"Why do you want to lock us up? We didn't do anything!
We don't even know how we got here!" Tracy cried.
"The queen has made a rule that strangers must be arrested
until there are more colors in the castle. The only way you two can be saved is
if you can make more colors for the queen," the tall guard said
"Tracy, we're going to get locked up forever!"
But Tracy wasn't scared."Take me to your queen," she said bravely.

The guards presented the girls to the queen.
The queen was a very fair woman, but she was also unmerciful.
"Your majesty, these two girls claim they can make colors that
will make our glorious castle even more beautiful,"
the tall guard said. The queen was very happy to hear this,
but she gave Tracy and Lily a warning.
If they didn't succeed, they would be locked up forever.

The guards took Tracy and Lily to three sad looking women.
"We are the queen's color makers. We have been locked up for years.
We have been unsuccessful in making new colors for the queen.
This is our last attempt,
and if we can't produce another color in two days'
time we will be locked up forever," one of the women said.

The only colors Tracy and Lily could see were the colors in the castle: red, green, yellow, and blue.
"Don't worry, we can help you make more colors from these colors. Then we can all be free," Tracy said. Lily didn't really believe her.

Tracy mixed the red and yellow together.
The two colors made orange. Everyone was surprised!
"Tracy, how did you do that?" Lily asked.
"I learned it at school.
There are lots of things we can learn if we pay attention in class,"
Tracy said. When she mixed blue and red together,
another color formed... Purple!

Tracy made a lot of colors, and the queen was very happy.

Now there were more colors in the castle,
the queen was so glad that she gave the two girls lots of presents
and told them to close their eyes.

When the two girls opened their eyes again, they were on the path
that led to their homes with their presents in their hands.
But this time around, they couldn't see the lake anymore.
It had vanished."Tracy, that was such an amazing adventure,
but we would have been locked up forever
if you hadn't known how to make colors.
I will be more serious about my studies from now on," Lily promised.
And from that day on, Lily did her best to keep her promise.

BLACK + WHITE = GREY
WHITE + RED = PINK
YELLOW + BLUE = GREEN
BLUE + RED = PRPLE
RED + YELLOW = ORANGE
RED + BLACK = BROWN